The Smile

MICHELLE MAGORIAN

The Smile

With illustrations by Sam Usher

Barrington Stoke

First published in 2015 in Great Britain by
Barrington Stoke Ltd
18 Walker Street, Edinburgh, EH3 7LP

www.barringtonstoke.co.uk

This story was first published in a different form in
Love Them, Hate Them (Methuen's Children's Books, 1991)

Text © 1991 Michelle Magorian
Illustrations © 2015 Sam Usher

The moral right of Michelle Magorian and Sam Usher to
be identified as the author and illustrator of this work has
been asserted in accordance with the Copyright, Designs and
Patents Act, 1988

A CIP catalogue record for this book is available
from the British Library upon request

ISBN: 978-1-78112-500-7

Printed in China by Leo

This book has dyslexia friendly features

To my sons

Contents

1   The Howler   1

2   Sunglasses in Bed   15

3   Silence   24

4   Nice Wallpaper   30

5   So Soppy   47

6   Snowflakes   59

7   Baby Brother   75

Chapter 1

The Howler

Josh dragged the covers up over his head. His baby brother's howls still pierced through his bedroom wall. They even made it past the pillow Josh had tunnelled himself under.

"Waaa!"

"Not again," Josh moaned.

"Waaaaa!"

Josh switched on his torch to look at the clock beside his bed.

It was 4.20 in the morning.

It had taken Josh nearly an hour to drift back to sleep after the last bout of wailing. He groaned. This was what torturers did when they wanted to get vital information from their victims. People needed sleep. Josh would have told anybody anything they wanted to know a long time ago.

The torturer in Josh's house was only 17 days old.

'If I don't get some peace soon,' Josh thought, 'my baby brother will be lucky to live to his 18th day.'

He stuck his nose out over the blankets.

It was still as black as pitch outside.

The bedroom door next to Josh's room opened.

The howl rose in volume and then faded as the door closed. Josh heard his father pad along the landing to the bathroom. Dad was on the morning shift at work that week. It was his first week back after the baby's birth.

Josh wanted to join his dad for a chat, but he knew his dad would have got up at the last minute so that he could have an extra five minutes' sleep. Not that he had much chance of that with the Howler.

For three hours Josh had listened as his parents took turns with Charlie. They had walked up and down the creaky floor, singing to him and talking to him. But it made no difference. Still he howled.

They were so desperate that they started yelling and blaming each other for the fact that the baby was awake.

"Look at us!" Josh's mother had shouted. "We're rowing in front of him. And he's not even a month old. I never wanted to do that!"

Then Josh's father interrupted her. "Shhh," he said. "Look at Charlie."

There was silence.

Their row had sent him to sleep.

"We'll have to think of something new to argue about the next time he won't stop crying," Josh's dad had said. And his mum had burst out laughing. And the baby had stayed asleep.

Josh had been listening at their bedroom door. When he was back in his room, he felt cut off from their secret world. There they were, the three of them, wrapped up warm together while Josh lay alone in the next room, forgotten.

He heard the front door close and all of a sudden the house was silent.

"At last," he muttered. "I can get to sleep."

Chapter 2

Sunglasses in Bed

Josh closed his eyes. He longed for sleep, but his eyes soon sprang back open.

Now it was the wallpaper that kept him awake. Even in the dark he could make out the large pink and yellow flowers which ran wild all over the bedroom wall.

Josh's parents had promised they would decorate his room, but when? His howling brother took up so much of their time. They didn't even have time to talk to Josh, let alone start stripping the ugly old wallpaper off the walls.

They hadn't even put up curtains for him.

Josh glared in the dark at the wooden boxes that were balanced on top of one another against the wall. They were crammed with his comics and books. Josh kept his clothes in open suitcases and a big bag on the floor and he used the rail in the cupboard for the string puppets his grandpa had handed down to him.

He didn't really mind the clutter.
It was the wallpaper which made the
room so bad. It must have been chosen
by someone who was colour-blind and
short-sighted. Every time Josh walked in
the door he wanted to put a paper bag
over his head.

His parents had ignored his cries for help. They were too wrapped up in getting everything ready for the new baby.

Josh had even worn sunglasses in bed to make his point about how bright the flowers were. But his mother thought he was just trying to be cool. His father was so busy putting in a new washing machine ready for the flood of Babygros that he didn't even notice.

Chapter 3

Silence

The move. That was another thing that made Josh angry.

His parents had said they needed more space for the new baby, so they'd moved house.

Josh had to leave the street he had lived in for as long as he could remember and the room which was his. And then his beloved brother decided to be born the day before Josh's birthday, which meant his party was called off. Even his puppet theatre was still stuck in the bottom of a box. And all because of his wonderful new brother.

"Do you realise," Josh said to his mother the night before, "do you realise this baby will be with us for years!"

His mother beamed. "Yes," she said.

She'd tried to talk Josh into helping look after Charlie, but Josh wasn't interested. He was still too angry with Charlie for what had happened to his birthday party. What had happened to his entire life in fact.

"Silence," he whispered to the ugly flowers on the wall. "Wonderful silence!"

He closed his eyes again.

It was no good. He had to find out why it was so quiet.

Chapter 4

Nice Wallpaper

Josh peered round the door of his parents' bedroom.

His mother was sitting propped up by the pillows on the mattress, which was on the carpet. They didn't even have a bed yet.

Charlie's Moses basket stood on a trunk at the end of the mattress. The basket was empty.

It didn't take long for Josh to find out what had caused the silence. His mother was feeding Charlie.

Mum looked up at Josh and smiled.
Her face was still pale and the bags
under her eyes looked very dark, but
she glowed. She looked so happy that
she could have been a lighthouse. A red
towel was hung over the lampshade next
to her to help soften the light.

As Josh stepped into the room from the cold landing, the warm air nearly knocked him over. It was like the greenhouses in Kew Gardens. They kept it that warm for Charlie.

"Did he wake you again?" his mother asked.

Josh nodded and ambled towards the bed.

"Come on," his mum said, and she nodded at the pillows beside her. Josh climbed in next to her.

His mum leaned her head against his shoulder. "Sorry I can't give you a hug," she said. "My hands are full."

"I can see," Josh grunted.

He looked at the tiny baby on the pillow on his mother's lap.

He'd been embarrassed the first time he had seen her breast-feeding Charlie. Now he was so used to it, the sight was like wallpaper. Nice wallpaper.

"You were like this once," his mother murmured.

"Mmm," Josh said. It was hard to believe he could have been so small and helpless. "You always seem to be feeding him," he told her.

"That's because his tummy is tiny," his mum said. "He can only take the milk in small doses and he's also learning to suck. There's a lot for him to take in and learn."

"I know." Josh gave a weary sigh.

"The first month is always the worst," his mother told him. "After that it gets better. Charlie will be more settled and ..."

"A month!" Josh burst out. A month of this and he would be a wreck!

"Poor thing," his mother said, with a soft smile. "Why don't you bring a sleeping bag in here if you get lonely?"

"I might as well," Josh said. "I can hear him every time he cries. Do I have to go to school today?"

"Not if you don't feel like it," Mum said. "I can send a note to explain."

"But Dad's gone to work, hasn't he?" Josh said.

"Yes."

"Then I suppose I'd better go," Josh said. "It's just I'd like to get some sleep."

"Wouldn't we all."

Josh gazed round at all the New Baby cards. They covered the tops of three chests of drawers.

Big bunches of flowers drooped in
vases among them and on the floor.

"How long will you keep the cards
and flowers?" he asked.

"I don't know," Mum said. "I still like to see them. And, anyway, clearing them away isn't a priority for me at the moment."

'Like my bedroom walls,' Josh thought. 'They don't seem like much of a priority, either.'

Josh and his mother fell silent and together they watched the baby sucking.

Chapter 5

So Soppy

When Josh woke two hours later, his mother had only just finished feeding Charlie. She had propped him up so he was sitting. She was holding his tiny floppy body with one hand and patting his back with the other.

Charlie seemed to be staring at Josh. He gave a deep burp.

Josh smiled and his mother saw him. It annoyed him to be caught out but it was funny that such a loud sound could come from someone so small. Charlie's farts seemed to shake his Moses basket. Sometimes he woke himself up with them.

Outside, the dawn was beginning to touch the sky.

"Josh," his mother said, "would you mind holding Charlie while I take a shower?"

"Oh, Mum," Josh began.

"Please," Mum said. "This may be my only chance before Dad gets home and then he'll be too busy cooking our tea to hold Charlie."

Josh sighed. He didn't seem to have much choice.

"Thanks," his mother said.

She helped plump the pillows up behind Josh and she didn't hand Charlie over until Josh was sure he was comfy. He leaned back, crossed his legs and put a pillow over his knees. Then Mum placed the baby on top of it.

"He won't wet me, will he?" Josh asked.

"I can't promise," Mum said, "but I don't think so. And anyway he'll wet the pillow first, won't he?"

"I suppose so."

Mum ruffled Josh's springy hair. "I won't be long," she said. "Promise. I'll turn the light off so he can doze off."

Charlie was still staring at Josh with wide eyes. A slow trickle of milk escaped from the corner of his mouth. Mum dabbed at it with a cloth. She kissed Josh on the cheek.

"Oh, Mum," he protested, "don't be so soppy."

She laughed.

Josh watched her stagger to the door. She had had less sleep than all of them. All of a sudden he felt ashamed that he had been so grumpy.

"Take as long as you like in the shower, Mum," he whispered. "Me and Charlie will be OK."

Chapter 6

Snowflakes

As Josh heard his mother turn on the shower, he looked around at the cluttered room.

The curtains had been left open. A street-light lit the bare branches of a tree on the far side of the road. Now and then a car drove past, but apart from that it was quiet and still.

It seemed that everyone in the street was asleep apart from Josh's family.

It seemed unreal to be sitting here warm in his T-shirt while the pink of a winter dawn spread over the sky. It had started to snow. Snowflakes floated and drifted past the window like feathers. They landed on the bare branches of the trees and melted.

Josh looked down at his 17-day-old brother as he lay in the crook of his arm. He was still staring up at Josh and frowning.

Josh swallowed. He had dreaded being left alone with Charlie and now here he was, stuck with him. He cleared his throat.

"I'm your brother," he told him. He felt a bit silly.

Charlie had such a hard stare that it made Josh feel funny. And he didn't like the frown. Frowns meant worry.

What on earth did a 17-day-old baby have to worry about?

Josh let his fingers glide across the frown. He stroked up from Charlie's small round nose and fanned his fingers out above the baby's brows to the dark hair which plastered his head.

"There," Josh whispered. "I'll stroke that silly old frown away."

'It's something to do,' he told himself. It would stop him getting bored. But the more he stroked, the more he got lost in his task.

Bit by bit, the frown lifted from Charlie's face and dissolved under Josh's touch. As Charlie's face smoothed out, his eyes closed.

Then it happened. Fast. Fleeting. But it happened and only Josh saw it. And it wasn't caused by wind because his baby brother had already burped.

A smile. A blissful, contented smile. It wasn't crooked – both corners of Charlie's mouth curved up. And then the smile was gone and Charlie was in a deep sleep.

In that instant, Josh was filled with a love for his brother that was so intense that it left a lump in his throat.

All of a sudden, sleepless nights didn't matter at all.

From the moment Josh saw his brother's smile, he vowed he would care for him. No one but no one would ever lay a finger on Charlie. If anyone dared hurt him, Josh would pulverise them.

If Charlie was in danger, Josh would rescue him. He would dive into icy waters to save him. He would climb mountains. He'd swing from the trees! He'd ...

And then Charlie farted and opened his eyes for a second before he fell back to sleep again.

Josh laughed.

'That'll teach me to get soppy,' he thought. But he still couldn't take his eyes off Charlie.

"Tomorrow," he whispered into his brother's ear, "I'll unpack my puppet theatre. For when you're older."

Chapter 7

Baby Brother

Outside the snow fell thicker and thicker. Josh smiled. He smiled so wide that his cheeks hurt and so deep that he forgot about clocks and called-off birthday parties and pink and yellow wallpaper.

Josh had something far better to think about now. He had his baby brother. He had Charlie.

Have you read all the Little Gems?

New!
COLOUR
Little Gems

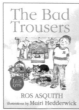

This
last o